Books by Clara Vulliamy

MARSHMALLOW PIE THE CAT SUPERSTAR

MARSHMALLOW PIE THE CAT SUPERSTAR: ON TV

*The Dotty Detective series
in reading order*

DOTTY DETECTIVE

THE PAW PRINT PUZZLE

THE MIDNIGHT MYSTERY

THE LOST PUPPY

THE BIRTHDAY SURPRISE

THE HOLIDAY MYSTERY

Marshmallow Pie the Cat Superstar

Clara Vulliamy

HarperCollins *Children's Books*

First published in Great Britain by
HarperCollins *Children's Books* in 2020
Published in this edition in the USA by
HarperCollins *Children's Books* in 2021
HarperCollins *Children's Books* is a division of HarperCollins*Publishers* Ltd,
HarperCollins Publishers
1 London Bridge Street
London SE1 9GF

www.harpercollins.co.uk

HarperCollins*Publishers*
1st Floor, Watermarque Building, Ringsend Road
Dublin 4, Ireland

1

ISBN 978-0-00- 846134-8

Clara Vulliamy asserts the moral right to be identified as the author
and illustrator of the work.
A CIP catalogue record for this title is available from the British Library.

Printed and bound in England by CPI Group (UK) Ltd, Croydon CR0 4YY

MIX
Paper from
responsible sources
FSC™ C007454

For Win, with much love

Map of my apartment

Shhh!
My secret stash
behind the sofa

Sofa is mainly for ME

My
cardboard
box →

My
toy box

Tv

Balcony for
relaxing in the
sunshine (and
annoying Buster)

Bathroom
(I do NOT
like water.)

Broom cupboard
(cosy)

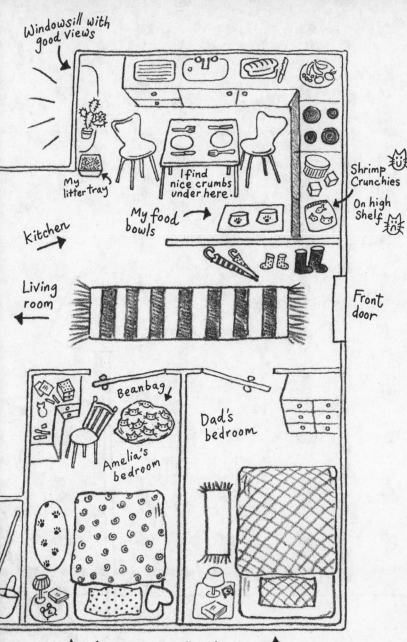

Windowsill with good views

My litter tray

I find nice crumbs under here.

Shrimp Crunchies

On high shelf

Kitchen

Living room

My food bowls

Front door

Beanbag

Dad's bedroom

Amelia's bedroom

(I'm not really allowed in the bedrooms but I sometimes sneak in.)

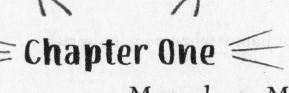

Chapter One

Marvelous Me

Oh, hello. Yes, you can come in, but you can't sit down because there's only room for me on this sofa.

I am a fancy cat. I prefer to be addressed by my FULL name, which is *Marshmallow Marmaduke Vanilla-Bean Sugar-Pie Fluffington-Fitz-Noodle.*

I'm not happy when people shorten it.

I pretend I haven't heard them, at first.

Here comes my human, *Amelia Lime.*

"Hello, Pie!" she says. See what I have to put up with?

I live here with Amelia and her dad
in a tiny top-floor apartment in
the middle of the busy city. I didn't
always, though.

The Early Years

Until not long ago I lived in a huge house in the country with Amelia's rich Aunt Julia, until she jumped into her private plane to fly around the world and couldn't take me with her. So I was popped into the back of a taxi and sent over to Amelia. I would be company for her, everyone said.

I like the easy life.

I spend a lot of time sitting in the sunshine on our little balcony.

There's a dog called Buster in the
apartment below. When he is out on
his balcony I look down on him, in
every way, which drives him CRAZY
and keeps me entertained for hours.

This afternoon Amelia throws down her school bag and excitedly rummages in her coat pocket. "Look—just look at this!" she says, pulling out a buckeye nut, a broken pencil, a hair clip shaped like a space rocket, and, finally, a crumpled piece of paper. I yawn, waiting for her to get to the point. "They were giving out these leaflets in **Pawsitively Purrfect** when I went in to buy your **Shrimp Crunchies**. . . ."

I can't help doing a little dribble. **Pawsitively Purrfect** is a very good pet shop, and **Shrimp Crunchies** are my favorite.

Amelia reads the leaflet aloud. . . .

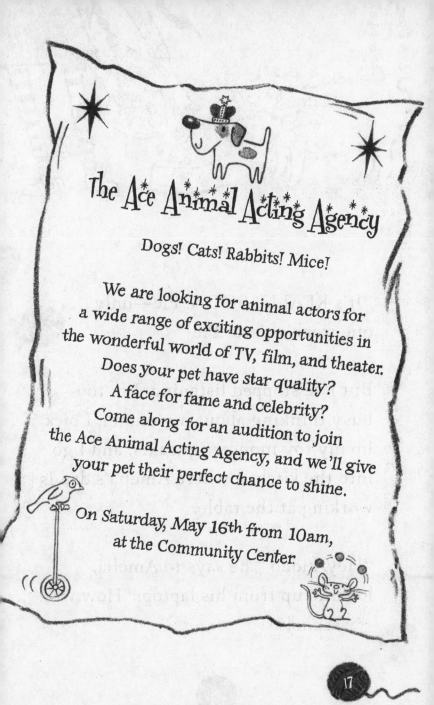

The Ace Animal Acting Agency

Dogs! Cats! Rabbits! Mice!

We are looking for animal actors for
a wide range of exciting opportunities in
the wonderful world of TV, film, and theater.
Does your pet have star quality?
A face for fame and celebrity?
Come along for an audition to join
the Ace Animal Acting Agency, and we'll give
your pet their perfect chance to shine.

On Saturday, May 16th from 10am,
at the Community Center.

"It's REALLY SOON, Pie—only one week's time! Pie?"

But I've stopped listening. I'm too busy thinking about my dinner. I pick up my toy mouse, Squeaker, and I go into the kitchen where Amelia's dad is working at the table.

"Hey, kiddo," he says to Amelia, looking up from his laptop. "How was school?"

"Hey, Dad," says Amelia. "Usual stuff."

I pace up and down impatiently while Amelia sorts the **Shrimp Crunchies** into my bowl. They come in yellow, pink, and white, but I will only eat the yellow ones.

Amelia's dad is reading her school newsletter while they eat their dinner together.

"Let's see if there's anything here you might like to do," he says. "Netball team tryouts?"

"I don't think so," says Amelia.

"Twinkle Toes Dance Club?"

"No way!"

"Well, how about this—why don't you enter the public-speaking competition? You can do it in pairs, it says here."

Amelia's cheeks go pink. "Oh no, that would be the WORST," she says. "Everyone would be looking at me, and I wouldn't be able to find a partner to do it with anyway."

She shows her dad the acting-agency leaflet. "This is loads better. I'd still get to do exciting things, but it would be PIE in the spotlight, not me. Pie deserves to be a HUGE star, and I'm going to help him!"

I only really hear the last bit, as I tend to zone out if the conversation isn't about me. A star? I feel like a star already, to be quite honest.

"We MUST give the acting audition a go," Amelia carries on when I've finished my dinner and I'm just giving my whiskers a quick clean. "They're sure to give you a place in their agency—they will love you!"

Of course they will. I lick a stray crumb that has got stuck up my nose. A class act, that's me.

While Amelia is brushing her teeth
at bedtime, I jump up onto the edge
of the bath and investigate an open
bottle of shampoo.

"We need to make sure you're looking
absolutely fantastic," she says, "and
take photos, make a business card, and
begin your TRAINING! Lucky it's
the weekend tomorrow, no school. . . .
We'll start first thing in the morning."

I give the bottle a little tap with my
paw.

"You will try your very best, won't
you? Pie?"

I don't answer. I keep tapping the
shampoo until it falls onto the floor.

S
p
l
a
t.

NICE.

Chapter Two
No Such Thing as Too Many
Sombreros

I'm just having a wonderful dream about finding a roast chicken twice as big as me, when Amelia wakes me up. So much for my usual lazy Saturday morning.

"I'm going to teach you some TRICKS for the audition!" she announces cheerfully, still in her pajamas and waving a hoop in the air.

"First we will practice jumping," she says.

Amelia ties a piece of string around Squeaker. Holding the hoop a little above the floor she slowly pulls

Squeaker through it. I'm meant to follow? Why on earth would I bother doing that? I stretch luxuriously and slump further into my cushion.

"Okay, let's try something easier," she says happily. "The high five!"

She has a ridiculously tiny piece of ham inside her closed hand and holds it up to me. As if I would raise a paw for that. HONESTLY.

"All right, we will do the simplest of all—polite sitting. It's very important to make a good first impression."

She holds the tiny piece of ham above my head. "Come on, Pie," she says.

"Sit up straight for a tasty snack!"

I look at the ham and I look at her. I close my eyes.

"Never mind! Let's leave all that for now." She smiles and gives me the ham anyway. I knew she would.

I go back to sleep. Hope I can find that roast chicken again.

When I wake up I see Amelia looking through my box of outfits. That's more like it—I always enjoy the chance to look even more FABULOUS.

"What would be best for your photo?" she asks. "One of these bandanas I made for you?"

"Sunglasses?"

"You have loads of different hats—so many sombreros!"

My Five Most Fabulous Hats

I was born with amazing
fashion sense. You either have
it or you don't.

I try on lots of alternatives,
but nothing is quite good
enough.

"This needs to be EXTRA special,"
Amelia says. She fetches her sewing
box and makes me a new sparkly
green bow tie.

"It brings out the color of your eyes,"
she says, holding me up to the mirror.

I agree. I look spellbindingly
handsome.

Before bedtime I go out onto the
balcony, hoping that Buster is out too.
He IS.

I've invented a hilarious new game to
annoy him. I sit in a position so that
I can hang my tail
down through the
railings and give
it a little twitch to
attract his attention.
He can see but cannot
reach. He barks loudly.
I give my tail another
wiggle. Buster jumps up,
his barking building to an
absolute frenzy, but still I
am out of reach.

From somewhere a voice calls out
"What is all that racket?"

"Keep the noise down!" calls another.

I hear Buster's human hurriedly
taking him inside.

HA.

Chapter Three

Stop BUGGING Me, Buster

Amelia is chatting about the audition while she combs and brushes my fur, getting me ready for my photo. "Just think—you could be famous!" she says. What I think is that it's all a big fuss about nothing. But I must say I have fluffed up magnificently.

She puts on my bow tie, and we set off for the photo booth in the post office. Amelia has to carry me down many flights of stairs because the elevator is broken.

OUT OF ORDER

On the way out we bump straight into
Buster and his human coming back in.

Buster growls and barks at me—
grrrrrrrrrrr-RUFF—tongue lolling.
How rude. I give a low hiss back, my
fur standing on end.

His human is laden with bags. "We've been shopping—LOTS of presents for Buster!" she says. She shows us their new multicolored crystal poop-bag holder, a golden bowl, and a Precious Pets blanket with his name embroidered on it.

"That's nice," says Amelia in a quiet voice.

"And Buster has so many skills," his human carries on. "I only take him to the very BEST classes!"

 Amelia looks down at her small coin purse and doesn't say anything.

But when we carry on up the road, Amelia says to me, "Don't take any notice. YOU have star quality—just you wait and see!"

We walk past the kiosk on the corner where Amelia and her dad sometimes pick up a coffee and a hot chocolate.

The kind lady who works there waves
out of the hatch.

"Hello, Amelia!" she says. "Ooh,
doesn't Pie look stylish?"

After that we feel great.

39

We arrive at the post office and squeeze into the photo booth.

Amelia pulls the curtain shut and puts in her coins. First the seat is too low . . .

then we are too close . . .

then I've had enough and try to leave . . .

but finally we get it just right.

"You look AMAZING!" says Amelia, showing me the photos.

I am a bit ruffled and my bow tie is askew. *That's Buster's fault*, I think crossly. But yes, despite that, I do look amazing.

We head home. Amelia carries me back up the stairs again, because the elevator is still broken.

Back in the apartment, while she helps her dad sort out the laundry, I get into my cardboard box. I am EXHAUSTED. Amelia pops the iPad in with me, and puts on my favorite show, which is *Woodland Birds*.

Then Amelia says, "Now I'm going to make our business card!"

There is only just room for her to sit at one end of the kitchen table and lay out her pens, paper, scissors, and glue. The rest is covered in bits of bicycle. Her dad has been tinkering with this EVERY weekend, but it never seems to be mended.

The minute she picks up her pen to begin, I realize I am bored, so I loudly meow to be let out onto the balcony.

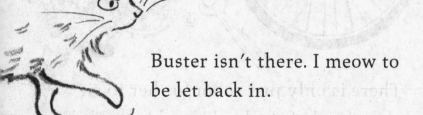

Buster isn't there. I meow to be let back in.

By this time, Amelia is getting on well with our business card. It looks pretty good.

"I can't fit your whole name on it," she says.

I give her a disapproving look.

"But just 'Pie' might not be special enough for this. . . ." At last she understands. "How about 'Marshmallow Pie', halfway between the two?"

I think I can just about tolerate that.

44

"Now for the finishing touch—your signature," she says. She dabs my paw onto a small ink pad, and gently presses it onto the card.

MARSHMALLOW PIE
Owned by Amelia Lime

Amelia rinses my paw in the sink.

"Scoot over!" says her dad, washing his bicycle-y hands with a funny green goo. Then he goes over to the fridge and peers inside. "Shall we have broccoli for dinner tonight, with . . . broccoli?"

"Broccoli is good," says Amelia.

While her dad is cooking, Amelia shows him our business card. "Wow— nice job!" he says.

"I just hope it does the trick," she replies. "This is Pie's big chance! I can't get cards specially printed, and he

doesn't have lots of expensive things. I
hope he'll still stand out. . . . "

"He will definitely be noticed," says
her dad, "especially as you've made
something personal. MUCH better!"

I go back onto the balcony. Still no
sign of Buster.

I'm fast asleep on the sofa when
I'm woken up by a commotion.
Humans get into such a panic
sometimes. Amelia can't find our
business card and is searching
everywhere for it. I can't possibly
help, so I carry on dozing.

She finds it at last. Underneath me.
No matter how small, if there's a piece
of paper, I'll sit on it.

Chapter Four
You Didn't See Any of This, Okay?

While Amelia is at school in the daytime and no one is looking, I take advantage of being home alone to express my *inner kitten*.

I chase my tail—a CLASSIC.

I pretend a speck of dust is a juicy mouse to hunt. Stare at it intently. Crouch down low with my bottom in the air . . .

and . . .

POUNCE.

I wrestle Amelia's slipper to the floor and fight it ferociously until its pompom falls off.

The pompom makes a great addition to my secret stash that I keep hidden behind the sofa. Socks, hairbands, a bus pass, a set of keys, Amelia's dad's missing glasses case. . . . Well, if people will leave things lying around, why shouldn't I borrow them?

I spend the afternoon trying to run up the curtain. When I was small I could reach the top of any curtain I liked, but these days . . .

not

so

much.

At least now there are some interesting new rips in the fabric to investigate, and loose threads to play with.

Oh, are you still here? Listen . . . my kitten games, my secret stash—this is all strictly private, okay? You mustn't tell ANYONE.

Every afternoon this week when Amelia gets home from school, she tries to persuade me into a new fitness routine to "get me into shape".

Really, what cheek. My shape is *EXCELLENT*.

Amelia's Workout Plan

Chasing ping-pong ball

The roll-over

The agility course . . .

I am so not interested. The thing is, if someone wants me to do something, I just don't want to do it anymore.

MUCH more importantly, over breakfast on Friday morning, Amelia's dad says to her, "Want takeout tonight?"

I spend all day thinking about it.

Takeout night is the BEST night. Amelia's dad comes in carrying a large paper bag full of delicious smells.

To make sure they don't forget about ME, I jump from lap to lap, meowing constantly—building up to more of a shriek—until I am given some prawn-cracker crumbs to lick.

Now I am trying to get inside the empty paper bag—backwards. Even though it's a little too small and my bottom bursts out of the other end, it is entirely dignified and not at all embarrassing.

After dinner, Amelia and her dad do the dishes together and chat about the audition tomorrow. I hardly bother to listen.

"The big day is almost here at last—
I'm very excited but SO nervous!"
says Amelia. "I really believe in
Pie and want everyone to see how
fantastic he is. But the thought of
going into a room full of people I
don't know—I'll feel very shy."

"Don't worry, you'll be brilliant!"
says her dad. "And luckily Pie has
enough confidence for both of you,"
he adds, chuckling.

I'm just dozing on the
sofa. I still don't think
this acting lark is
worth all the huge
amount of effort
I'm putting in.

Before bedtime I take Squeaker out onto the balcony. I can hear that Buster is out too. I go over to the railings and look down. But . . .

DISASTER.

I open my mouth to meow at him and drop Squeaker. He falls down onto the balcony below.

I look on in absolute horror, unable to do a single thing about it.

Buster reaches out a paw and pulls Squeaker close toward him.

The last I see of my precious toy is him disappearing into Buster's happy, dribbly hug.

Chapter Five
Lights! Camera! Action!

"I've been awake for HOURS!" says Amelia.

She is already dressed, with a bag packed, fidgeting restlessly by the front door. I see she's wearing a sparkly green ribbon in her hair that matches my bow tie.

I wander over to my food bowl. I
never hurry breakfast.

I look around for Squeaker, before
remembering last night's calamity.

Amelia's dad is giving us a lift to the
audition and will wait for us in a café
opposite. We sit in the back of the
car. Amelia has a peppermint to stop
her feeling sick. I curl up on an old
blanket and have a cosy catnap.

When we arrive it's already really
busy. Amelia gives our names to a
young man at the front desk. He has a
little beard, round blue-tinted glasses,
and a clipboard. "Hi, guys. I'm Dexter,"

he says. "Take a seat and we'll call you
when it's your turn." Amelia takes our
business card out of her pocket and
bravely hands it to him. Dexter raises
an eyebrow and gives her a small smile.

I sit on Amelia's lap and look around.
I see animals of every kind and size,
some in carrying cases, some on
laps, some tearing about the room
or trying the lavish selection of free
snacks. And, oh boy, the snacks are
INCREDIBLE.

Maybe this isn't going to be so bad
after all.

There is a massive dog with black spots and a grumpy expression, and a tiny dog wearing a ridiculously frilly fairy dress.

There are two tufty guinea pigs under a blanket nibbling a celery stick.

As names are called out, people take their pets over to a raised stage at the end of the room to be filmed and photographed.

Audition Hopefuls

I watch a sausage dog who can skateboard, a fancy rat pushing a tiny shopping cart, and a parrot who can whistle "Jingle Bells".

"Everyone is so good and trying so hard!" says Amelia.

I'm not worried. I relax and have a few more Tuna Tasties.

Sitting next to us on one side is a big, fluffy white rabbit. She has *Daisy Darling* embroidered on her woolly hat and a constant supply of carrot sticks.

On the other side there is a boy about the same age as Amelia with an orange kitten on his lap. The kitten keeps trying to attract my attention, pouncing on my tail and batting me with her tiny paws. Infuriating.

"Sorry about Gingernut," he says.
"She gets very overexcited. I'm Zack,
by the way. Amelia, isn't it? I think
we're in the same grade at school!"

Amelia goes pink, but manages to
smile and say, "Yes, I think we are!"

I ignore Gingernut for as long as I can,
but when she starts actually chewing
my tail I give her a swift sideswipe.
It makes no difference whatsoever.
Kittens these days. Honestly. SO badly
behaved.

We wait and wait.

Daisy Darling is called up . . .

Then the tiny dog in the frilly fairy
dress . . .

And at last it's my turn.

Dexter calls out, "Marshmallow Pie to
the stage, please!"

"Hope it goes well!" says Zack.

Amelia carries me over to a high
stool. I can feel her racing heartbeat.
"Good luck!" she whispers. "You'll be
brilliant!"

She gives me an encouraging smile.

So here I am, under the bright
lights, with everyone looking at me.
Okay, so I must admit it IS quite
fun. I could get used to this. All I
have to do is sit here, rewarded with
snacks, and everybody marvels at my
awesomeness.

"Ready for your close-up?" the photographer says to me, and I am just gazing gorgeously into the camera when something familiar catches my eye, coming in through the door. I know that nose, those googly eyes, that walk.

Buster.

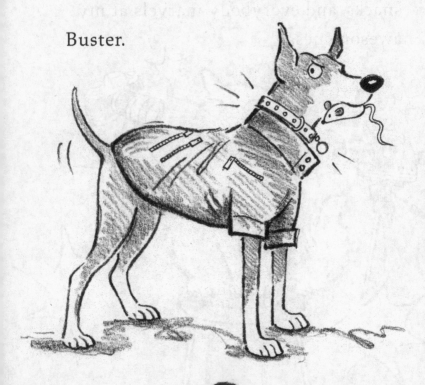

Clean, smoothed, and glossy. He has clearly been to the Groom Room at the back of **Pawsitively Purrfect**; I recognize the smell of their peppermint shampoo. He is wearing a leather jacket and a shiny new collar, and he's carrying Squeaker in his mouth.

Heads start to turn away from me as people watch him arrive.

I am **FURIOUS**. The NERVE, turning up here after stealing my beloved Squeaker. Now he's trying to steal the attention of my adoring crowd. I do NOT want him here.

This isn't show business . . .

I flatten my ears back and, hissing,
leap off my stool and through the air.

HISSSS!

HISSSS!

I don't land as hoped on Buster but
feet first into a food bowl, sending
meaty biscuits flying everywhere. The
bowl skids away across the floor, taking
me with it, until we crash against a
chair and I tumble out into a heap.

There are gasps of horror.

"What dreadful behavior!" mutters one person in the crowd.

"Dreadful! Dreadful!" repeats the whistling parrot.

Amelia looks devastated. "But . . ." she begins. Her voice trails away.

As I get to my feet, Dexter and the photographer are talking quietly together, shaking their heads. I see Dexter crossing something out on his clipboard.

By now everybody is staring at Amelia. "Some people clearly can't keep their pets under control," says a woman nearby, not noticing that her dog is rummaging through the trash can in the corner, snout stuck in a paper coffee cup.

Buster catches my eye as he walks past. The shine from the silver studs on his new collar is dazzling.

"Oh, what a shame, your audition— **RUINED!**" says Buster's human over her shoulder as she leads Buster coolly up to the stage.

Amelia bursts into tears, runs over to grab me, and we rush out of the door.

Chapter Six
Buster's Beefy Chews

"It was AWFUL," Amelia is saying to her dad as she puts our matching bow tie and hair ribbon back in the box. "I hated it when everyone stared at me. And it was all for nothing—since the audition went so badly wrong nobody knows what a star Pie could be. Nobody believes in him."

"*You* do," says her dad.

"Yes, I really do. It was just bad luck Buster coming in right at that moment. I think Pie is the best cat in the whole world, but other people never got to see. His chances of fame must be pretty much zero now. . . ."

She looks at me. I'm busy trying to reach a **Shrimp Crunchie** that has rolled under the fridge.

"I just really thought this was our chance for something big."

Her dad gives her a hug, but I barely notice.

Nearly . . . nearly . . . GOT IT!
CRUNCH.

The next few days are very dull. Amelia is really quiet. I don't go out at all.

One afternoon, when Amelia's dad is taking out the recycling and the front door is open, I can just hear Amelia on the stairs coming home from school. I can hear Buster and his human too, coming out of their apartment below.

"Oh, hello," she is saying to Amelia. "I'm sure you'll be overjoyed to hear—Buster's audition was a HUGE success! I've just bought him a new bed shaped like a sports car to celebrate. Anyway, I can't stand here chatting—busy, busy!"

Amelia doesn't say anything. She carries on slowly up the stairs to our apartment.

Who needs a sports car bed? **RIDICULOUS**. I go over to my cosy cardboard box. It has one of Amelia's old sweaters in it, which smells nice and comforting. (But don't tell her I said that.)

Later I meow to be let out onto the balcony. I look down and see Buster. He can't be that thrilled with his new bed—he mainly seems to just want to cuddle Squeaker.

I blame Buster for everything.

Another humdrum week goes past. I see a bird on the windowsill. I find a leaf. Not much else happens.

On Friday afternoon, Amelia's dad asks her, "What would you like to do this weekend?"

"I don't know. . . ." she says. "Now that Pie's hopes are dashed, I just feel we haven't got any nice things to look forward to, or places to go. I'm so disappointed for him."

"Why don't you hang out with some friends from school?" he suggests.

"But Pie is my best friend," says Amelia.

I'm on the balcony again when Amelia comes out to tell me it's dinnertime. Then she gasps and points across to a nearby building. "Oh, LOOK!" she says.

There, all lit up, is a MASSIVE photograph of Buster on a poster advertising **Beefy Chews** dog food.

I am so annoyed. Not only is everything HIS FAULT and he has Squeaker—now I have to see his huge face all the time too.

We go back inside and Amelia closes the curtains.

Then she sorts the **Shrimp Crunchies** into my bowl. I tuck in with loud enthusiasm, but I notice she barely touches her own food.

She plumps up my cushions and tidies my cardboard box but hardly says a word.

She brushes my fur but stares into the distance.

I give her a side-eyed glance. And it
dawns on me properly for the first
time . . .

My human is sad.

So I feel sad too.

I've been blaming everything on
Buster. But maybe it's my fault as well.

Chapter Seven
The Old Razzle-dazzle

I get up early on Saturday morning, giving up sleeping in, which is something I would only ever do in an EXTREME emergency. I find the original Ace Animal Acting Agency leaflet in my secret stash behind the sofa and leave it just outside Amelia's bedroom door.

When she wakes up she finds the leaflet. I watch her sitting at the kitchen table, reading it and chewing her fingernail nervously.

I jump up on the table—carefully stepping over the bits of bicycle—and give her an encouraging nose bump.

"Do I dare?" she says to herself.

She plucks up the courage and bravely phones the agency.

At first there is no answer. Then the line is busy. She looks anxious as she keeps trying the number, waiting and waiting . . .

Until finally she gets through.

"Can I speak to Dexter, please?" she says, her voice shaking a little.

Another long wait . . .

Then at last Dexter is on the line.

"It's about my cat, Marshmallow Pie," she says.

"Oh yes, I remember him!" Dexter chortles.

"I know we messed up," Amelia begins, "but if you would only give him another chance. . . ."

Dexter is unconvinced. "I'm sorry, but I really don't think he's ready for acting work. Look, I've got to go—I'm getting ready for another day of auditions."

But to my surprise, after she puts down the phone, Amelia has a very determined look on her face. "We have to go there," she says. "We have to try again. Come on, Dad! Into the car, everybody!"

As soon as we arrive, Amelia goes straight over to Dexter, carrying me.

"This is Marshmallow Pie," she says in a loud voice, "and he's really amazing and fantastic and I know he's going to be a HUGE STAR!"

Dexter looks startled. The photographer lowers her camera and stares at us. An assistant steps forward to ask us to leave.

But Dexter speaks first. He says to Amelia, "Well, you're loyal and you stick up for your cat—I like that. But, honestly, his audition—it was completely wacky!"

"It will be so much better next time, you'll see!"

"Hmmmm. I'm really not sure. . . ." says Dexter.

But then he seems to think of something. He rummages in a folder

and pulls out our handmade business card. "Yes, I remember noticing this at the time," he says, studying it closely. "It's pretty cool—different and creative."

He looks at us both. "I must admit, you're an unusual pair!"

There is an agonizing silence. Amelia grips me tightly. I can tell she is holding her breath.

"Okay," says Dexter. "Show us what he can do."

I behave beautifully in my second audition. I sit SO politely,

jump gracefully
through the hoop,

and give Dexter
the PERFECT
high five.

Of course I could ace it all along—did
you ever doubt me?

As it is all going so well, I give it a bit of the old razzle-dazzle too.

My Cool Moves

The photographer is smiling and Dexter is writing notes on his clipboard. I can see that Amelia has her fingers crossed on both hands, even though she hides them in her pockets.

"I'll let you know," Dexter tells Amelia when it's time to leave.

In the car on the way home I snuggle up to Amelia. Just to allow her to express her affection for me, of course. Don't think I'm getting all soppy.

She strokes between my ears and pets me under the chin.

"We make a great team, Pie!" she

says. "And that's what I wanted more than anything. I'm really proud of you!"

She is SO happy. And I'm purring quite loudly myself.

Chapter Eight
Fame at Last

The phone rings. I ignore it. Amelia and her dad are talking excitedly in the kitchen. When I realize they are talking about me, I open one eye.

Amelia bursts in. "Pie! PIE! It worked! The agency has taken you on and you've been cast in the Snow White detergent magazine advertisement! Daisy Darling had to drop out because she has a cold, so they needed another fluffy white animal URGENTLY. This is your

BIG CHANCE!"

I yawn and stretch, playing it cool. I am not in the least surprised. It was only a matter of time. I do give a small happy chirrup, but that's only because I see a leaf outside; it has nothing to do with any of this.

yaawwwwwwwwwh...

"Dexter said they like you just the way you are," Amelia tells me, "and that your sometimes unpredictable behavior is all part of your showbiz personality."

"Well done, both of you!" says her dad. He is attaching a basket to Amelia's bicycle, which—a miracle—is now finished. It looks very nice with a fresh coat of green paint.

"The photoshoot is tomorrow," Amelia carries on. "We have so much to do. But first. . . ."

She empties the entire contents of her money box into her coin purse. "Come on, Pie—we're going to **Pawsitively Purrfect** to celebrate!"

We head out. We don't even have to take the stairs as the elevator is working again. Which is just as well, because Amelia is taking her bicycle. I sit in the basket. I have no intention of exerting myself.

On the way, as Amelia pedals along, everybody seems to be smiling at us.

We stop at the kiosk on the corner so that Amelia can tell the kind lady our news.

"Oh, how wonderful!" she says. "I'd like a signed photograph to pin up, please, so all my customers can see!"

Just as we arrive at **Pawsitively Purrfect** we bump into Gingernut's human, Zack, coming out with a can of kitten food.

"Hey, Amelia!" he says. "How did it go with Pie and the agency?"

Amelia goes pink and smiles. "It went really well in the end—he's been cast in a magazine advertisement!"

"AMAZING! Huge congrats!" he replies. "They've taken on Gingernut too—I'm just waiting to hear the details."

"That's fantastic!" says Amelia.

Amelia buys me a bag of **Shrimp Crunchies** (extra large) and a new toy mouse stuffed with catnip. I decide I will let Buster keep Squeaker, as for all his expensive stuff he doesn't seem to have much in the way of toys to cuddle up with.

Best of all, Amelia buys me a lime-shaped charm on a sparkly new green collar. You can come closer and admire it, if you like. I look stunning.

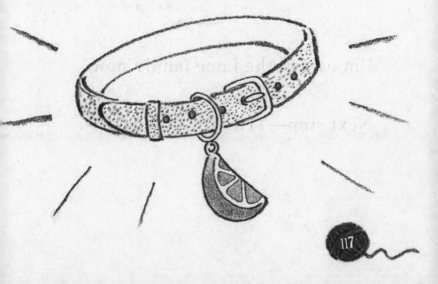

I'm part of the Lime family now.

Next stop—THE LIMELIGHT!

The End

Look out for Marshmallow Pie's next adventures!

Marshmallow Pie the Cat Superstar on TV

Clara Vulliamy

Marshmallow Pie the Cat Superstar in Hollywood

Clara Vulliamy

Coming soon

Check out more of
Clara's books . . .

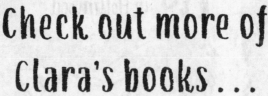

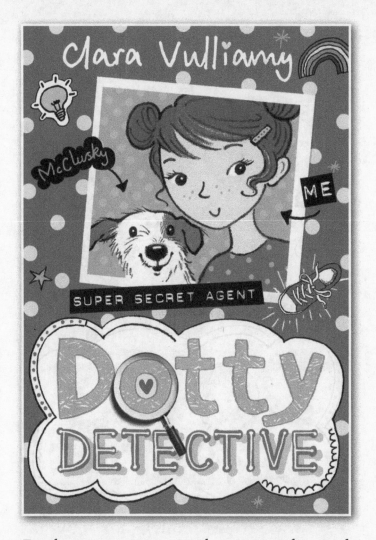

Dot loves super-sour candy, running fast, and solving puzzles. With the help of trusty sidekick Beans and top dog, McClusky, she is always ready to sniff out a mystery! So when someone seems set on sabotaging the school talent show, Dot is determined to save the day. . . .

When Dot starts hearing strange noises at
night, Beans is convinced there has to be
something SPOOKY afoot. But, before they
can be certain, Dot and Beans must GET
PROOF. . . . Easier said than done when the
suspect appears to be invisible!

Dot and Beans can't wait for their school trip
to Adventure Camp where they will do lots of
exciting adventure activities and may even win
the Adventurers' Prize! But why is someone
trying to spoil the fun?

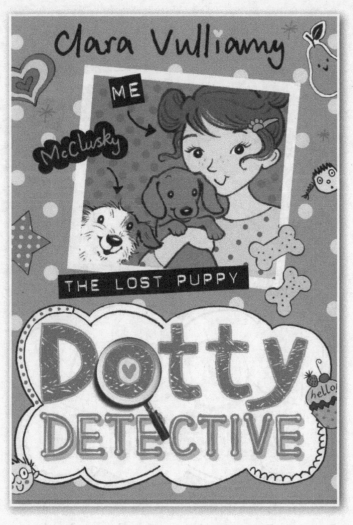

There's a fantastic surprise at the school gates—
Dot's friend Joe has brought along his new
sausage dog puppy, Chipolata! She is SOOO
cute! But then she goes missing. Can the Join the
Dots Detectives track down the lost little dog?